¡CHANA!

4 LIVE FROM CEDAR HILLS

Other Avon Camelot Books in the
¡CHANA! *Series by*
Michael Rose Ramirez

(#1) ¡*HOLA*, CALIFORNIA!
(#2) HOPPIN' HALLOWEEN
(#3) GINGERBREAD SLEEPOVER

Avon Books are available at special quantity discounts for bulk purchases for sales promotions, premiums, fund raising or educational use. Special books, or book excerpts, can also be created to fit specific needs.

For details write or telephone the office of the Director of Special Markets, Avon Books, Dept. FP, 1350 Avenue of the Americas, New York, New York 10019, 1-800-238-0658.

¡CHANA!

4 LIVE FROM CEDAR HILLS

MICHAEL ROSE RAMIREZ

Illustrations by Marcy Ramsey

This is a work of fiction. Names, characters, places, and incidents either are the product of the author's imagination or are used fictitiously. Any resemblance to actual events, locales, organizations, or persons, living or dead, is entirely coincidental and beyond the intent of either the author or the publisher.

AVON BOOKS
A division of
The Hearst Corporation
1350 Avenue of the Americas
New York, New York 10019

Interior illustrations by Marcy Ramsey
Produced by Judy Gitenstein
Published by arrangement with the author
Visit our website at **http://AvonBooks.com**
Library of Congress Catalog Card Number: 97-93868
ISBN: 0-380-79021-1
RL: 3.5

First Avon Camelot Printing: January 1998

CAMELOT TRADEMARK REG. U.S. PAT. OFF. AND IN OTHER COUNTRIES, MARCA REGISTRADA, HECHO EN U.S.A.

Printed in the U.S.A.

OPM 10 9 8 7 6 5 4 3 2 1

Para Ramon Ramirez,
mi abuelo fantástico y
el mejor compañero de cuarto
en el mundo

Dear Reader:

You will find Spanish words and phrases used throughout the text in this book. Usually, you'll be able to tell what each word means by the way it is used in the story. But when you aren't sure, you can look up the word or phrase in the glossary found at the back of the book.

¡Siga leyendo! Read on!

Michael Rose Ramirez

4 LIVE FROM CEDAR HILLS

One

It all started on a Sunday night when a surprise storm covered Cedar Hills with more than a foot of snow. Cedar Hills was in California, tucked up in the northeastern corner of the state near Oregon and Nevada, and it got plenty of snow each winter. But no one expected that much snow so early in November.

The morning after the storm, Chana Millán and her friends at Binghamton Elementary School decided to build a snowman.

"It will be the biggest snowman ever," Nikki Thayer said.

"A giant snowman—as big as the whole playground," Stephanie Jordan said.

"El Gigante," Chana called it. "The Giant."

"The Fourth-Grade Giant," Joy Selzer said.

Pretty soon, Amanda Cole, Adam Zimmerman, Teddy Tully, Skyler Hughes IV, Scott Hurley, Valerie, Gordy, and most of Chana's other classmates joined in. Everyone rolled the large bottom section next to the slide. They climbed onto the ramp and piled snow onto the middle section. They made the snowman bigger and bigger until it really was a giant.

"We'll be in the *Guinness Book of World Records,*" Scott yelled.

On Tuesday their principal, Mrs. Watson, announced that Sonny Day, the weatherman for Channel 11, was coming to Binghamton. He was going to do a story on the biggest snowman Cedar Hills had ever seen.

Now it was Wednesday and Chana figured she and her classmates might really become famous. "I'm gonna be on TV!" she said as soon as she woke up. She was out of bed, dressed, and running out of her room in a matter of minutes.

"Ay, cálmate," Mrs. Millán called as Chana zoomed by her parents' bedroom. "Calm down."

Chana slowed to a bounce and took the stairs two at a time. She burst into the kitchen where her father was standing at the stove with a spatula in his hand.

"I had a feeling you'd be up early this

morning," Papi said with a smile. "And I'm making the star of the family her favorite breakfast."

"*¡Órale!*" Chana said. "Right on! Bull's-eyes!"

Papi had invented Bull's-eyes one morning when Chana was little. She had folded a slice of bread in half and bitten into it. When she opened it, there was a hole in the center. Papi had put the bread in a pan and fried an egg in the hole. Chana told her father that the fried egg in the middle of a piece of bread looked like a dartboard. Since then, they'd called them Bull's-eyes.

Now Papi had gotten fancy and used a cookie cutter to make perfectly round holes. He toasted the little circles of bread that were left over, and Chana and her older sisters, Cindi and Clara, ate them with butter and jam.

Chana's sisters were fifteen and they were identical twins. "But they're as different as pineapples and *paella*," their Uncle Ray liked to say.

As Chana put six place settings around the table, Cindi stepped into the kitchen. "Good morning, TV celebrity," she said to Chana with a wink.

Cindi yawned and sat down in the breakfast nook. "Smells great, Papi," she said.

"Oh, this is wonderful, Hector," Mrs. Millán said as she came in and joined Papi and the girls at the table.

"Hey, don't you all have any manners?" joked Uncle Ray from the doorway. He rubbed sleep from his eyes and then squeezed into a spot at the table. "Save me some!"

Chana's whole family didn't always get to have breakfast together. They had only moved to Cedar Hills two months earlier, in September, and they were still settling in. Chana had lots more homework now that she was a fourth-grader. The twins were sophomores at Linwood High School and already had boyfriends. Chana's father had started his job as a history teacher at the state university and her mother worked as a physical therapist at St. Augustine's Hospital. Uncle Ray, Mom's baby brother, worked as a housepainter.

Chana's parents had always wanted a house and they had saved for a long time in their *barrio* in New York. Then Mr. Millán had been offered the job at the university and they had moved to Cedar Hills. Chana loved living in a big house instead of the tiny apartment they had all shared in New York. She especially liked having a yard where her cats, Flaca and Sparky, could play.

After the family had devoured every last bite of Papi's Bull's-eyes, they got their things together for work, school, and the exciting morning with Sonny Day. Mr. and Mrs. Millán had said they would go to their jobs late so they could see Chana and her classmates with Sonny Day and the Giant. They had also said the twins could get to their school late since it was a special occasion.

"Camera, film, batteries," Papi was saying as he checked his camera bag.

"Bundle up. It's cold out today," Mrs. Millán reminded them, and Chana walked to the hall closet to get her mittens and earmuffs.

Chana was rummaging through the closet when she heard Uncle Ray say, "I'm sure glad I don't have a painting job today. I wouldn't want to miss this." He pulled his coat from the rack in the hall and put it on.

"Well, Ray, seems you haven't had a painting job in several days," Papi said, sounding annoyed. He shoved a stack of exam papers into his briefcase. "And this isn't New York. People have houses here, not apartments. You can't paint houses in the snow."

"*¡Caramba!* You know I can paint the inside of houses during the winter months, Hector," Uncle Ray said.

Chana wondered if her father and uncle were going to fight. She had found her mittens and earmuffs in the hall closet and put the earmuffs on so she wouldn't have to listen. When Mrs. Millán came into the front hall and saw Chana with the earmuffs on she turned to Papi and Uncle Ray and said, "Didn't you two have this same argument last night?"

Chana looked from her mother to Papi, then back again, as though she were watching a tennis match. Mrs. Millán was smiling, but Papi wasn't smiling back at her. As Chana turned back to her father he answered his wife. "Yes, Carmen," he said. "We did. But we're all getting settled here in California now, except for Ray. He's twenty-three years old, after all. It's time for him to go back to school or to get a steady job."

"Now, listen," Uncle Ray said, his voice rising. "I'm getting settled, too. Just give me some time. And don't forget, I've always managed to help with the bills . . ."

Chana couldn't stand it when anyone in her family was in trouble or fighting. She remembered Papi and Uncle Ray arguing about

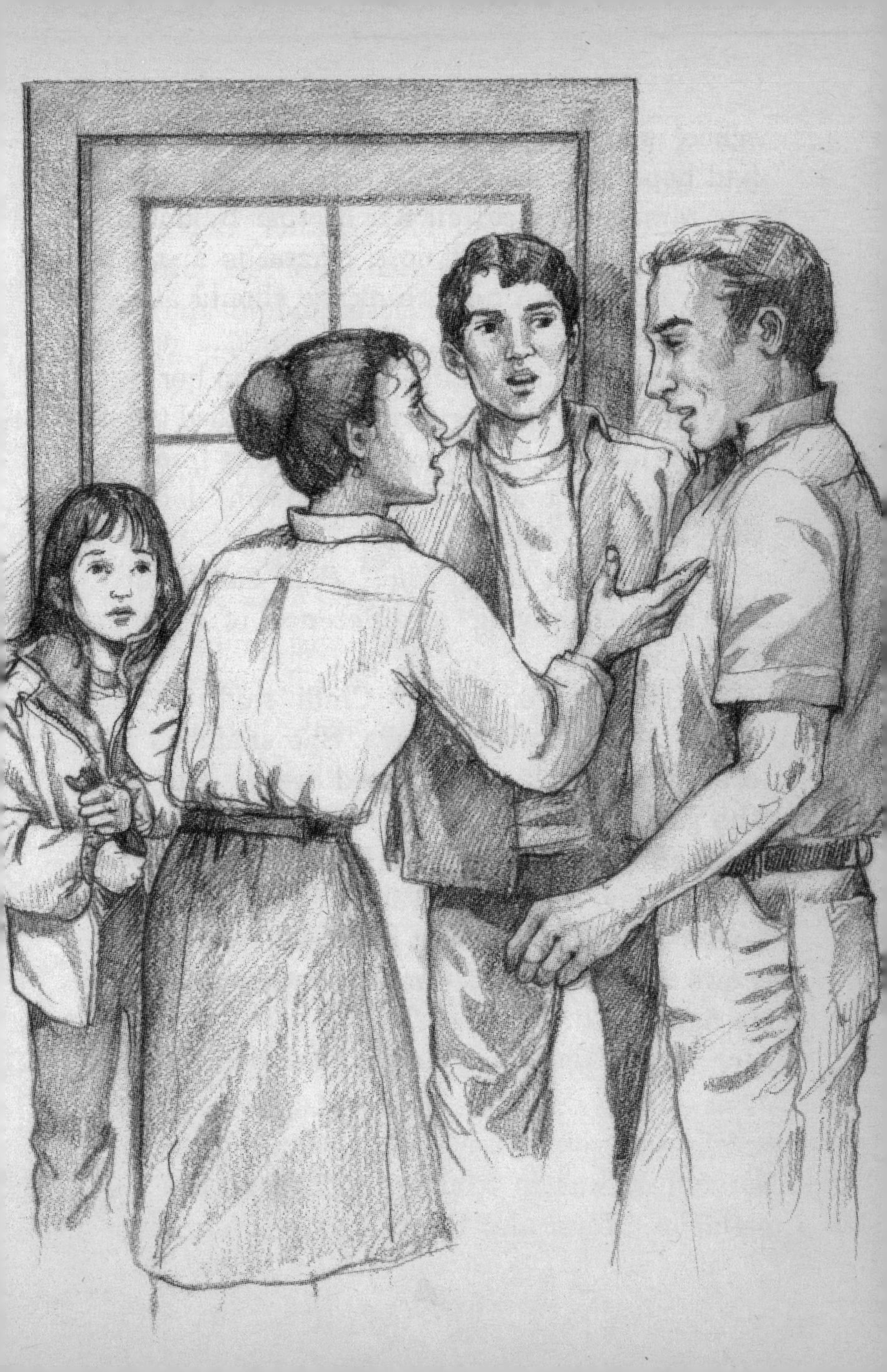

school and work back in New York, but she had hoped it would stop when they moved.

Mrs. Millán cut off her brother by holding up her hands. "Right now, Chana is about to be on television and I think we should all get going," she said firmly.

Chana shifted from side to side on her feet. She had taken the earmuffs off and stood twisting her mittens in her hands. Looking from her father to her uncle, she said, "Yeah, don't be mad at each other."

"We're not mad, *hija,*" Papi said gently. "We're just having a difference of opinion, that's all."

"Okay, c'mon then!" Cindi said, coming down the stairs with Clara. She snatched her coat off the rack and ushered everyone toward the garage. Chana hoped it was just a difference of opinion. She could hardly wait to meet Sonny Day. She wanted to be with her friends and show off their Giant and see herself on the news. And she didn't want her father and uncle to fight.

The Channel 11 weather van was parked right in front of Binghamton Elementary School. Television crews, cameramen, photographers and news reporters were busy setting up their equipment. The Cedar Hills *Herald* was also there to cover the story.

As Mr. Millán steered the car into the parking lot, Chana saw kids from other grades running everywhere. Dozens of parents, teachers, family members, and friends were taking pictures, drinking coffee or hot chocolate from paper cups, and waiting anxiously for Sonny Day to arrive.

When Papi parked the car, Chana jumped out and ran to the playground where her teacher, Ms. Young, was rounding up the fourth-graders.

"Please gather around your snowman, children," Ms. Young was saying. "Sonny Day should be arriving any minute now."

Chana squeezed in beside her four friends who called themselves the Squinkles. Just as Chana said hello to Joy, Nikki, Stephanie, and Amanda, another Channel 11 van pulled into the parking lot. Painted on the side of the van were the words "Make Today A Sonny Day." The crowd buzzed with excitement.

"Chiiildrrren!" Mrs. Watson chirped above the commotion. "Here he comes!" She skipped around the students with her necklaces and bracelets jingling out of her winter coat. Her rings flashed against the bright snow and her black and gray hair bobbed up and down, making her earrings shake and shimmer.

Sonny Day stepped out of the van and waved as he made his way across the playground. When he saw Mrs. Watson, Ms. Young, and the Giant with all the students around it, he turned to the cameraman beside him who had just finished setting up.

"Good morning, I'm Sonny Day coming to you live from Binghamton Elementary School in Cedar Hills. I'm here with the biggest snowman I've ever seen," he began. He tilted his microphone to Ms. Young and asked, "Who created this incredible work of art?"

"Well, my fourth-grade class made it all by themselves," Ms. Young said with a smile.

Sonny Day walked over to Adam and Skyler, who were standing in front of a huge snowball resting near the Giant's right foot. "Did you boys roll this snowball?" he asked.

"Yeah. It's a soccer snowball. We made it together," Adam said proudly.

"Just perfect," Sonny Day said as he made his way over to Chana and her friends.

"Hi there," he said to Stephanie. "What's your name?"

"Stephanie Jordan," Stephanie answered.

"Well Stephanie, how many kids do you think it would take to go around this big guy?"

Stephanie tugged at a strand of frizzy brown hair sticking out from under her hat and said into the microphone, "Lots, I bet."

"Why don't we find out?" suggested Sonny Day. He picked some students and had them surround the Giant in a circle. It took nine kids holding hands to go all the way around the snowman's body.

"That's your giant's girth," Ms. Young said to the class. "Girth is the distance around something."

Sonny Day faced the camera and said, "Seems the Binghamton fourth-graders *snow* all about math!" When he turned back around he looked at Chana and asked, "Does this snowman have a name?"

"Sure!" Chana said. "I named him *El Gigante.*"

"The Giant, right? Well, it suits him," Sonny Day said.

"Yep, just like the Giant in Puerto Rico," Chana said, grinning from ear to ear into the camera.

"I didn't think they got much snow in Puerto Rico," Sonny Day said with a smile, and tipped the microphone back to Chana.

"They don't," Chana said. "But there used to be a man, a real giant, who lived in a town called Carolina. They even named a basketball team after him, *Los Gigantes*, and a mall and other stuff."

"Is that so? In that case, you could call your snowman Mr. *Caroline,*" Sonny Day suggested.

"Yeah, and maybe we could sing Christmas *Carols* for him!" Chana said.

Sonny Day laughed heartily into his microphone, putting his arm around Chana's shoulders. He turned to the camera with Chana right beside him and concluded with, "This is Sonny Day, Channel 11, in Cedar Hills. Back to you, Margo."

Microphones clicked off and the crew started packing its gear. Chana turned to Stephanie and said, "Wow! That was fun! But I should have said something about the Squinkles."

"It's okay. We got to be on TV!" Stephanie said.

"And you were fantastic," a voice near Chana said.

The girls turned and saw a tall woman walking toward them. She was wearing a bright red baseball cap with "THE CEDAR HILLS HERALD" and "J.J." stitched on the front. She held a notepad and pencil in her hand. Amanda, Joy, and Nikki stopped talking and turned to see what was going on.

"My name is Jan Jarvis," the woman said with a smile. "I'm a newspaper reporter. What are the Squinkles?"

"We're the Squinkles," Chana said, pointing to herself and her friends.

"How did you come up with that name?" Jan Jarvis asked.

"We picked it from the word *escuincles,*" explained Stephanie.

"It means "little kids" in Spanish," Chana said. "But anyone can be a Squinkle."

"Yeah," added Nikki. "It's not a private club or anything."

"You don't have a special handshake or a secret password?" Jan Jarvis asked.

"No," Joy said. "It's just friends."

"Hey, I like that. Now, I know you're Stephanie," the reporter said, nodding at Stephanie. "What are each of your names?" she asked the others

Nikki, Joy, and Amanda each told Jan Jarvis her name. When it was Chana's turn she said, "My name is Sanjuana Millán but my *apodo*—I mean my nickname—is Chana."

"Chana Millán. That's a very unusual name. I take it from what you said to Sonny Day that you're Puerto Rican," Jan Jarvis said.

"*Sí ¡Y orgullosa!* Yeah, and proud of it!" Chana said.

"Well, Chana, you should be proud of that," Jan Jarvis said. "You know," she continued, "I came by today to report on the big snowman for the *Herald*. When you mentioned Puerto Rico, it occurred to me that you'd be perfect for another article I have in mind."

"Really?" Chana said.

"Really," said Jan Jarvis. "I'd like to do a whole story on you and your family."

Just then, Chana's parents, the twins, and Uncle Ray came over.

"You did great in front of the cameras, Chana," Uncle Ray said.

Jan Jarvis introduced herself to Chana's family and explained her idea to everyone. "As you know," she said, "there are quite a few Mexicans in California, but I don't think there are many Puerto Ricans. A lot of Hispanics live in the larger cities, but communities are also diversifying up here in the north. I'd like to introduce all of you in our special Sunday section called New Faces in Cedar Hills."

Chana's family liked the idea. *"¡Qué nice!"* exclaimed Mrs. Millán.

Jan Jarvis asked each member of the family several questions about New York and their move to California. She asked everyone about their hobbies and about work and school. Papi gave Jan Jarvis his office phone number at the university so they could make plans for her to come and interview and take photos of the family in their new home.

"And what do you do for a living?" Jan Jarvis asked Uncle Ray.

"I'm a . . ." Uncle Ray began.

"Famous drummer!" Chana finished for him. She had seen her uncle and Papi exchange a serious look. Chana didn't want Jan Jarvis to think her family should be in the Fighting Faces section instead of the New Faces section.

"Great, I've got lots of good information here. Oh, what's the correct pronunciation of your last name?" Jan Jarvis asked Uncle Ray.

"Me-yahn, kind of like million," Uncle Ray explained.

"Got it," Jan Jarvis said, closing her notebook.

A moment later the bell rang and Jan Jarvis said, "Hey, how do you say, 'See ya later, alligator' in Spanish?"

"¡Nos vemos, cocodrilo!" Chana and her sisters said together. Jan Jarvis chuckled and the Squinkles raced toward room 7. Chana's parents and the twins said good-bye and before Uncle Ray left he whispered to Chana, "A famous drummer?"

Chana laughed and Uncle Ray added with a smile, "Thanks for stopping a public argument. You're one in a million, kid."

"You mean, one in a Millán!" Chana called over her shoulder as she sped after her friends to class.

Three

It was time for math, and once Ms. Young got the class to quiet down, she gave them a real lesson on how to measure the girth of things.

When math was over they had their once-a-week music class. Chana loved to play the cymbals. She crashed and banged them as loud and as often as she could. Sometimes their music teacher, Mrs. Roy, would say, “I dare say, can’t hear anyone else now, can I?”

Mrs. Roy was from England and Chana loved her British accent. She liked the way Mrs. Roy called Chana and her friends chums. If they hadn’t already decided on calling themselves the Squinkles, Chana might have suggested the Chums.

After music class Chana asked Mrs. Roy if she could take the cymbals home to practice. Mrs. Roy said she could and signed a pair out for her. "Practice makes perfect," she said as Chana picked up the cymbal case and headed for her next class.

The last class of the day was reading, and Chana wasn't looking forward to it. There were two reading groups and Ms. Young, or Ms. Old as Chana sometimes called her, had put Chana with the Robins. The more advanced group, the Swallows, was where Chana thought she should be. She loved to read and she didn't think it was fair that she was in the Robin group. "We're going to talk to Ms. Young about it at our parent-teacher conference," Chana's father had promised her.

Chana finished her reading assignment early and looked out the window at the snow-covered playground. She hoped it would snow that night so the Giant wouldn't melt.

When the bell rang, Ms. Young dismissed the students for the day.

Chana walked home with Amanda. They walked slowly, laughing and playing in the snow. Chana was in no hurry to get home today because she was worried about Papi and Uncle Ray fighting.

When they reached Amanda's house, Amanda said, "Well, see you later. I mean, *adiós*."

"Hey, you'll be speaking Spanish in no time!" Chana said. Stephanie and most of the other kids loved it when Chana taught them Spanish words.

"Oh, no, I'm just learning," Amanda said. "Did I make a mistake already?"

"No way. *Pronto*, pretty soon, you'll be as good as Stephanie," Chana said.

Amanda wasn't an original Squinkle like Stephanie, Joy, and Nikki. When Chana first moved to Cedar Hills, Amanda and her mother had been unfriendly to Chana. Cindi said she thought it was because they didn't like Hispanic people. Mrs. Millán had encouraged Chana to try and be friends with Amanda. Chana didn't want to fight with her and had given a doll she made to Amanda's baby brother, Justin, as a kind of peace offering. She loved sewing and making things, especially the dolls her father's mother, Grandma Leonor, had taught her to make.

Chana figured that the doll had helped because now she and Amanda were getting to be friends. Mrs. Cole hadn't become as friendly as Amanda, but as Mrs. Millán said, "Change doesn't happen overnight. Be patient, *mija.*"

Chana was just finishing a T-shirt for Amanda with "Viva La Squinkles" stitched on it like the ones she had made for the other Squinkles. The shirts were purple because that was Stephanie's favorite color. They also said "Don't Bug Us" at the bottom because Joy loved bugs.

Chana and Amanda said good-bye when they reached the Cole house. When Chana got to her house, the twins were sitting in the kitchen talking about their boyfriends. Clara was sipping mineral water while Cindi drank a glass of chocolate milk and munched on potato chips.

Cindi handed the bag of chips to Chana and, as if reading her mind, she said, "Don't worry, Papi's not home yet and Uncle Ray is in a good mood. Everything is peaceful, Chana. Hopefully, they finished their fight this morning."

Chana was relieved. She ate a handful of chips, then wiped her hands on her jeans and took her cymbals out of their case. She crashed the cymbals together as she stomped around the house pretending to be in a marching band.

Cindi shouted, "Hey, I thought you liked peace and quiet!"

"Just peace," Chana shouted back.

"*¡Cállate!*" her mother called. "Quiet! Please play those things in the garage."

Mrs. Millán was home from work and she was upstairs on the phone with Jeannie, her friend from work. Uncle Ray came out of the living room making a time-out sign with his hands. "Chana, that's no Latin rhythm I've ever heard! How 'bout I give you some real music lessons. Would you like that?" he asked when she had stopped.

"Sure!" Chana said.

Uncle Ray could sing in the sweetest voice Chana had ever heard, and he could play all kinds of instruments. His favorite was the drums. He had a drum kit set up in the garage, and Chana had been wanting to learn how to play ever since they'd moved.

Uncle Ray helped Chana put the cymbals back in their case. In the garage, she walked slowly around the drum set. She touched the shiny cymbals and ran her fingers along the sparkling red tom-tom shells. Uncle Ray lowered the stool so she could reach the bass drum pedal and Chana sat at the set. Then her uncle handed her a pair of drumsticks.

Chana was banging and crashing and just getting warmed up for her lesson when her mother opened the garage door.

"Papi's home with the pizza, you two drummers," she said.

"We'll finish our lesson later," Uncle Ray said.

"*Seguro que sí.* Definitely," Chana said, and they went inside to join the family for dinner.

When Chana and her uncle sat down Cindi said, *"Buen provecho,"* and began passing around the salad bowl.

"They say, *'bon appétit'* in French," Papi said, raising his glass of soda in a toast.

"And, *'buon appetito,'* in Italian," said Mom, reaching for a steamy slice of the pizza and a napkin at the same time.

"They say, 'dig in,' at my boyfriend Mark's house," Clara said.

"We say 'good luck!' at the cafeteria at school," Chana teased, wrapping a long piece of cheese around her fork as she freed a slice from the pizza.

During dinner everyone talked about how exciting Sonny Day's visit had been and about Jan Jarvis coming to do a story on the family.

Then the twins told everyone how they were planning to fool their boyfriends the next day.

"We're going to dress the way we usually do," Cindi explained. "Then after school we're going to switch our outfits in the gym before we go over to Beaver's Burgers to hang out."

"Yeah, and when we get there, I'll be Cindi and she'll be Clara," Clara said with a giggle.

Papi chuckled and their mother shook her head. "One of these days you two are really going to get into trouble with your tricks," Mrs. Millán said.

"No way!" Cindi and Clara said at the same time.

Chana told her family about how she couldn't wait to get out of the Robin reading group.

"You're a great reader," Chana's mother said proudly.

Papi agreed, and as he finished his third slice of thick-crust California-style pepperoni pizza, he said to Uncle Ray, "You've always been great at math, Ray. A teacher in the mathematics department at the university mentioned to me that she's always looking for tutors who are good at math and who get along well with children. She runs an after-school program to help elementary-school kids with their arithmetic homework. I think you'd fit the bill perfectly."

Chana saw Ray give her father what looked to her like an angry glance. "Oh no, not this again," she said under her breath.

Four

Uncle Ray stood up, took his plate, and dropped it with a loud clatter into the sink. "I've got a job, thanks," he said to Chana's father.

"Doing what?" Papi asked.

"May I be excused?" Chana asked quickly. "Uncle Ray's going to finish giving me a drum lesson."

"Drums!" Papi said. "Ray, we really need to talk. You are too smart to be wasting your time. You can't make a living playing music. That's just for fun. You need something to fall back on—an education. *La educación es fuerza.* You need your own place to live, you need a steady job . . ."

"I've got a place to live and I've got a steady job," Ray said gruffly.

"Painting houses isn't a job," Papi answered in the same tone.

"Papi . . ." Chana began.

"Yes, Chana, you may excused. No drum lessons for now. You have homework to do."

"But . . ." Chana said.

"You heard your father," Chana's mother said, kissing Chana's cheek. "We're going to talk down here for a little bit."

The twins looked at Chana and each of the girls put her plate in the sink. Together they went upstairs to the twins' room and closed the door.

Chana sat on Cindi's bed next to Cindi and fought back the tears she felt filling up her eyes. "Why's Papi so mad at Uncle Ray?" she asked her sisters.

"He just wants him to finish college and get a good job," Cindi explained.

"He has a job painting houses," Chana said. "And he's a musician, too."

"You know how important school is to Mom and Papi," Clara said.

"I guess," Chana said.

"*¡La educación . . . es fuerza!*" all three sisters said at once, rolling their eyes and giggling. It was an expression they'd heard from their parents "about a zillion times," as Clara always said.

"I know, I know. Education is strength.

But Papi said Uncle Ray should get his own place," Chana protested. "What if he leaves?"

"Uncle Ray's been living with us for as long as I can remember," Clara said. "He's not going anywhere."

Chana hoped more than anything that her sisters were right. She stood up and went into her own room where her cats, Flaca and Sparky, were waiting for her on the bed.

"*Estoy preocupada.* I'm worried," Chana said as she stroked Flaca's fluffy tail.

When Chana had finished her homework, she sat in her rocking chair by the window to sew. She figured that finishing Amanda's T-shirt would help take her mind off her uncle and her father. It helped a little, and when it was done, she went downstairs to her uncle's room. She knocked softly on his door.

"*Pásale.* Come on in," Uncle Ray called.

"Uncle Ray," Chana said, handing him a wrinkled slip of paper. "I've got a coupon I want to cash in."

"So you have," he said, taking the paper.

Uncle Ray didn't make much money as a housepainter, so whenever he had gifts to give, he gave coupons. Chana had coupons promising "Unlimited hugs upon request," "Three chores done for you—Limited offer only," and one that said "One tickle-free week—no expiration date."

"Well now's a good time to cash this in," Uncle Ray said, turning a coupon that said "Good for one free trip to the ice cream shop" over in his hands. "We should celebrate this morning's television appearance," he said.

"Can we?" Chana asked.

"Of course," Uncle Ray said. "*¡Vámonos!* Let's go!"

Chana and her uncle bundled up and told Chana's mother where they were going. Before they left, Mom said to Uncle Ray, "Chana can stay up late tonight to wait for the news at ten. Don't be late."

"No problem," he said as they stepped outside. They rattled downtown in his secondhand pickup truck. At Arnold's Candy and Ice Cream Shoppe, Chana and her uncle sat at a large round table. Since it had begun to snow again they decided to split an Arnold's Blizzard Wizard.

Chana and Ray listened as Arnold described his concoction: "It's got six scoops of vanilla ice cream with coconut shavings, bananas, and marshmallows. I top it with white-chocolate sauce, white chocolate-chip-cookie

Today's Flavors

pieces, macadamia nuts, whipped cream, and vanilla sprinkles. What do you say, kids?"

"We'll take it," Uncle Ray said and winked at his niece.

When they had eaten every last bit of the Blizzard they wiped their mouths on their sleeves.

"Mom and Papi never let me do that at home," Chana said.

"Well, you can do it here. This is a nag-free night—for both of us," Uncle Ray said, and he didn't give Chana a napkin.

"Chana," he said after they had stopped laughing. "I know you're worried about me and your dad. But I want you to remember that we're *familia*—we'll work things out between us. Now, we're here to celebrate the Squinkles' television debut, right?"

"Right!" Chana said.

They clinked their mugs of creamy hot chocolate together and then sat a while longer and talked about Chana's next drum lesson. Uncle Ray promised he would give her one the next day after school.

As they climbed down from their stools, Chana slipped her hand into her uncle's. They swung their arms as they walked back to his truck.

As they rumbled home Chana watched the windshield wipers brush away the falling snowflakes. She wished she could wave her arms and brush away the fighting.

Chana and Uncle Ray made it home just as the news was starting. When the piece on the Giant came on Papi clicked on the VCR. Chana sat mesmerized in front of the television set.

"Live from Cedar Hills . . . it's Chana Millán!" Uncle Ray shouted when Sonny Day appeared on the screen.

"¡Cállate!" everyone shouted. "Quiet!"

"That's us! That's really us. Not on a home movie—really for real on real TV," Chana said.

"That's right," Clara said. "You're a famous Squinkle."

"My girl is going to be the talk of the town," Papi boasted.

"The family in New York and Puerto Rico is going to love Papi's tape of this," Mom said.

"¡Híjole!" Chana cried when the television screen was filled with the close-up shot of her and Sonny Day just before he concluded the segment. "That was the greatest!" she shouted.

"Well, you've had a long day, little one," Chana's mother said.

"It's late now and way past your bedtime."

Chana kissed everyone good night and went upstairs to her room. After a few minutes her mother came in.

"What should I dream about, Mommy?" Chana asked her.

"Let's see," her mother said, petting Flaca and Sparky who were nestled on either side of Chana. "Today's been full of good things and fun things, exciting things and new things."

"And worry things," Chana added with a yawn. "Like differences of opinion."

"Yes. And worry things," Chana's mother said quietly. "But you don't have to dream about those. Dream about . . . drums," she said. And Chana curled around her cats and hummed herself a lullaby—a Latin rhythm she made up all by herself.

"The penny! Ray, the penny!

Chana's mother was standing at the kitchen door with her hands cupped around her mouth, shouting down the empty hallway.

"Mom, *¿qué pasa?*" Chana said, getting up from the breakfast table and going over to her mother.

"Carmela, what's going on down here?" Papi asked as he hurried down the stairs. He always called Chana's mother Carmela, instead of Carmen, when he knew that she was excited about something. Papi stood looking from Chana to his wife as he adjusted his tie for work.

"Chana, didn't you just tell me your uncle gave you a knife?" Mrs. Millán asked.

"Sure, Mom," Chana said. "But don't worry, I'm not going to cut myself with it. It's a pocket knife—for drum repairs. It's on a key chain that has a special key on it called a drum key, for tuning drums. Uncle Ray's going to show me how to use it after school today when I have my drum lesson."

"Where did Uncle Ray go?" Mrs. Millán asked Cindi. Cindi had walked out to the hallway from the kitchen with Clara right behind her.

"Ray knows you can't give someone a knife as a gift unless you give them a penny with it," their mother explained.

Papi, Chana and the twins looked at one another with knowing glances. Now they understood. Mrs. Millán was very superstitious. She also knew a lot of home remedies. Even though they usually worked, Chana, her sisters, and their father liked to tease her. Standing in the hallway, they rolled their eyes and laughed.

"Don't mock the Mommy!" Mrs. Millán said, pretending to scold all of them. "A penny for a knife. It's true."

Uncle Ray walked down the hall toward the kitchen where they were standing. "She's right," he said, winking at his sister and smiling at the others. "Don't worry, Carmen, I remembered. I just went to my room to find a penny for Chana."

Uncle Ray opened his hand so she could see the penny in his palm. Mrs. Millán let out a sigh of relief and she and the twins went back into the kitchen. Papi shook his head and started up the stairs to finish getting ready for work.

"It's for good luck," Uncle Ray explained to Chana. "A knife symbolizes strength, but also danger because it can do harm. Some people believe you should give a penny when you give a knife. It reverses the bad luck so nothing unfortunate, like a severed relationship, happens."

"I guess that makes sense," Chana said, taking the penny from her uncle. *"Gracias, Tío,"* she said with a kiss.

"Por nada. You're welcome," Ray said. "When you and your sisters are ready, I'll give you all a ride to school."

Fifteen minutes later, the girls met Uncle Ray at the front door.

"Bye Papi, bye Mom," Chana called. To her sisters she said, *"¡El último que llegue es un huevo podrido!* Last one to the truck's a rotten egg!"

Chana plowed across the snow-covered lawn with her uncle and the twins making their way behind her. When they got to the truck they all jumped in and squeezed inside the cab.

When Uncle Ray dropped Chana off at Binghamton, he said, "See you after school for your drum lesson."

"For sure," Chana said.

In room 7, everyone was talking about seeing themselves on the news until Ms. Young said, "Class, we had a wonderful day yesterday and I'm very proud of all of you. But right now, it's time to get back to our studies."

Everyone settled down to work on the assignments for the morning.

After school, Chana and Amanda walked home together. Chana had finished the T-shirt that said "Viva La Squinkles" on it. She had it in her backpack and wanted to surprise Amanda when they got to her house.

"Want to come in for some cookies?" Amanda asked when they got there.

"Sure," said Chana. This was the first time she had been into Amanda's house.

Inside, the girls hung up their coats and

Mrs. Cole called, "Amanda, I'm in the kitchen feeding Justin."

"Oh, hello Chana," she said, looking surprised, when the girls stepped into the kitchen.

"Hi Mrs. Cole," Chana said.

"Would you two like a snack?" she asked, spooning strained vegetables into Justin's mouth.

"Yeah," Amanda said. "But not what he's having!"

Mrs. Cole chuckled as she put a plate of gingersnap cookies on the table and filled two glasses with milk.

"Thanks. Do you have any ice?" Chana asked.

"Whatever for?" Mrs. Cole asked.

"I like ice in my milk," Chana explained.

"Oh, okay. Is that something they do in Puerto Rico?" Mrs. Cole asked.

"No," Chana said. "I just like it that way."

"I see," Mrs. Cole said, and brought some ice for Chana. Chana thanked her, took a sip, then opened her backpack and took out the T-shirt for Amanda. Amanda wiped the crumbs from her fingers, then held the shirt up and said, "Wow, it's super!"

"What's all this I keep hearing about the

Squinkles?" Mrs. Cole asked her daughter. She took the T-shirt and examined it carefully.

Amanda explained to her mother what the Squinkles were and how Chana had picked the name.

"Jan Jarvis, from the Cedar Hills *Herald*, said she thought the Squinkles were great," Chana added.

"And she's going to write about Chana's family," Amanda said. "In the New Faces in Cedar Hills section."

"How nice," Mrs. Cole said. She put the shirt down and returned to spooning food into Justin's mouth. "And you certainly sew well."

"Thanks," Chana said, gathering her things. "My *abuela*—I mean, my grandmother—showed me how. Well, I guess I'd better go now."

"I'm glad you stopped by," Mrs. Cole said.

"See you in school tomorrow, Amanda. Thank you for the snack, Mrs. Cole," Chana remembered to say as she was leaving.

Chana walked home thinking about how rude Mrs. Cole had been to her when she had first moved to Cedar Hills. She was glad things were different now. Mrs. Cole had been friendly and even seemed to like the T-shirt she'd made. Chana decided her mother had been right and that change just takes time. She was glad she had waited.

"Yep," Chana said to herself as she bounced up her porch steps, "Things are peaceable. Just the way I like them."

Six

Mrs. Millán was home from work. When she came downstairs after changing her clothes, Chana told her the whole story of how she'd been invited in for cookies at Amanda's.

"Mrs. Cole was nice. She even said I sew well," Chana said.

"*Bueno*. Good," said Chana's mother with a smile. "You certainly are my little peacemaker. Maybe you can work your magic here with your dad and Uncle Ray."

Chana didn't think she could stop her father and uncle from fighting. "Mom, I don't understand what the big deal is about jobs and college."

"You're right," her mother said. "You

shouldn't be worrying about those things now. The two of them will work it out."

"That's what Uncle Ray said. He said since we're *familia*, we're supposed to work stuff out. So how come they're taking so long to do that?" Chana asked.

"Sometimes it takes time," her mother explained. "Be patient, sweetheart."

"Okay. I was patient with Mrs. Cole and today she was friendly," Chana said.

"See?" said Mrs. Millán. "Now listen, Papi and I have a surprise for you tonight and I need to run into town to buy some pastries. Why don't you come along and help me pick some out?"

"Sure!" Chana said. "Tell me what the surprise is."

"Chana," said Mrs. Millán, "if I did that, it wouldn't be a surprise."

"I guess not," said Chana, and she and her mother laughed and chatted as they headed for the store.

In town, they went to the bakery and Chana picked out her favorite Italian pastries and some cupcakes. They ran some more errands, and on their way home Chana told her mother that shopping made her hungry. So they talked about what they wanted for dinner.

"Cupcakes!" Chana said.

"I don't think so," said her mother. "Those are for after dinner."

"How about *tostones*?" Chana said, smacking her lips at the thought of *tostones*—fat, green bananas, or *plátanos*, twice fried in oil.

"Your favorite," her mother said with a smile. "And how about some pork chops and red beans and rice to go with your *tostones*?"

"¡Qué rico!" Chana said. "Yum! That's Uncle Ray's favorite too."

By the time they arrived back at the house Chana and her mother were both starved. Mom walked into the kitchen, expecting to find Papi home from work, Cindi and Clara home from school and their after-school activities, and everyone excited about the surprise she and Papi had planned. Chana was expecting to have her drum lesson with Uncle Ray before dinner. But that's not at all what happened when they went inside.

What they saw was Uncle Ray storming out of his room. "All this nagging is the last straw. I've had enough," he muttered.

"Enough of what?" Chana asked. "Not drums, I hope."

"Chana," he said, "I can't give you a drum lesson today."

"But you promised!" Chana said.

"I'm sorry, Chana. We'll talk about it later," Uncle Ray said as he picked up a duffel bag that was on the floor by the front door.

"Ray!" Chana's mother said. "You're not leaving are you?"

"I have to Carmen," he said. "I can't stay here with Hector. He just never lets up."

Before Chana could try and convince him to stay, Cindi and Clara charged through the front door.

"You kissed my boyfriend!" Cindi was shouting at Clara.

"I was pretending to be you. That's what we agreed on, remember?" Clara shouted back.

"Yeah, we were supposed to trick them, but that didn't mean you were supposed to go kissing my boyfriend," Cindi snapped back.

"It was just part of the joke, Cindi. Lighten up!" Clara said.

Mrs. Millán said, "Time out, everyone. Ray, wait a minute, please." Then she turned to the twins and said, "What is going on here?"

"I'm sorry, I can't wait," Ray said. He kissed Chana's cheek, nodded at the twins, then went out the door and got into his truck.

"Where's he going?" Cindi asked.

"He's moving out," Papi said, coming down the stairs. "And I'm going for a walk."

Papi took his coat from the closet and went out the back door.

"Has this whole family gone *loca*?" Clara said.

"You're the only *loca* one, Clara," Cindi fumed. "What kind of person kisses her sister's boyfriend?"

"*¡Ay!*" Clara said. "I'm going for a walk with Papi."

"Well, I'm going over to David's. He didn't think it was too funny when he realized he was kissing you. I hope he's still talking to me!" Cindi said. She stormed out in the opposite direction.

Mrs. Millán put her hands on Chana's shoulders and turned Chana to face her. "Listen, Chana," she said. "I need you to stay here for a little while by yourself while I go try to talk to Cindi. I don't want her wandering around out there, angry and cold. It's getting late."

"Okay," Chana said, not sure what to think about everyone in her family arguing and stomping out of the house at once.

"I'll be back soon," her mother assured her. "Don't worry."

Mrs. Millán kissed Chana, then stuffed her house keys back into her purse. She set out after Cindi, who had already gone down the street and rounded the corner toward David Andolino's house.

When the door closed behind her mother, Chana flopped onto the sofa and let out a huge sigh. She was deep in thought when she was startled by the doorbell. Chana ran to the window and peeked out through the curtains. Jan Jarvis stood on the Milláns' porch with a camera around her neck and a notebook in her hand.

Chana opened the front door.

"Hello!" Jan Jarvis said in a perky voice. "Your mom and dad invited me to interview you and your family tonight over dinner. My editor thought it was a great idea—you know, warm, close-knit Hispanic family enjoying a family meal together . . ."

Chana led Jan Jarvis into the empty living room, listening quietly as she rattled on and on. This is the worst night ever! Chana was thinking to herself. She's not going to see a warm, close-knit Hispanic family tonight—she's not going to see anyone at all!

Jan Jarvis continued talking as she set her

camera and notebook on the coffee table then took a seat on the sofa.

"Your dad said he was going to come home early and help cook dinner. He told me he loves to cook. He even said one of his brothers, Ricardo I think, works as a cook in San Diego. Now that's something! Here I expected to find a traditional family, but well, I guess this is the new generation . . ."

"Um, Ms. Jarvis," Chana interrupted. "I don't think we're having dinner tonight."

"Oh, no. Has something happened? I hope everyone is okay," Jan replied in a worried tone.

"Well," Chana said, trying to figure out where to begin explaining. "See, my dad and my uncle are fighting because my uncle's really a painter, not a famous drummer, and my dad wants him to go to college. My twin sisters are mad at each other because they were trying to play a trick on their boyfriends but Clara ended up kissing David and Cindi thinks she shouldn't have but Clara says Cindi should lighten up. So now my uncle left and my dad went for a walk with Clara and my mom went out to find Cindi who is trying to find her boyfriend to try to explain why Clara kissed him.

But we're really a very peaceable family—honest!"

Once Chana had finished, Jan Jarvis looked at her. "Oh my," she said. Then she chuckled and began to gather her things. "I guess I'll call your dad tomorrow and see if we can reschedule," she said.

Chana walked her to the door and on the porch Jan Jarvis said, "Well, see you later alligator. No wait, *¡nos vemos, cocodrilo!*"

After Chana had locked the front door, she returned to the sofa and sat fiddling with her knife and drum key. She thought about everyone fighting and realized she was angry, too. She was angry at her uncle for promising to give her a drum lesson and then leaving. And she was angry at Papi for making him leave.

Flaca jumped up onto Chana's lap. Chana scratched the cat's ears and rubbed the knife in her hand. "Education is strength and knives are strength. So if everything is so strong, why is everyone fighting?" she asked Flaca. Flaca purred and rolled over on her back so Chana could scratch her belly.

"Flaca," Chana went on, "Mom said I might be able to work my peacemaking magic on this family. But how can I do that? I don't have time to sew anything before everyone gets home." She sighed and Flaca stretched, twitched her tail, and repositioned herself on Chana's lap.

"Hey," Chana said after a minute. "I've got an idea! I'm going to reverse all the bad luck that's around here so there's no severed relationships." She slipped her knife back into her pocket, lifted Flaca from her lap, and ran upstairs.

Seven

In her room, Chana rummaged through her closet until she found the old coffee can where she collected treasures she found. She dumped everything onto the floor—marbles, tangled string, seeds, bottle caps, smooth pebbles, paper clips, sparkling bits of metal, broken toy pieces, and coins.

From the pile, Chana picked four shiny pennies. Then she went around the house and on each pillow—Papi's, Uncle Ray's, Cindi's and Clara's—Chana placed a penny. "A penny for good luck," she whispered with each one. Next, she went downstairs and started peeling the skins off three green bananas she would use to make her *tostones*.

Not long afterward, Mom and Cindi returned. Chana's mother was pleased that Chana had started getting dinner ready. After she and Cindi hung their coats, they helped Chana fix the rest of the meal.

Cindi was still upset and no one felt like making pork chops with red beans and rice. Instead, they prepared Chana's *plátanos* and heated up leftover pizza from the night before. As they cooked, Chana told her mother that Jan Jarvis had come by.

"Oh, no," Mrs. Millán said with a sigh. "That was the surprise! Papi and I had arranged to come home early and start getting everything ready. *¡Dios mío!* My goodness, what must she think?"

"It's okay, Mom," Chana said. "I explained everything to her and she said she'd come back another time."

"Everything?" Mom asked in a worried tone. But before Chana could tell her mother what she had said, the phone rang. Mrs. Millán answered and when she was finished she told the girls it was Papi.

"He said he and Clara walked into town and they're going to eat at the diner. They'll be back later."

"I guess Uncle Ray won't be back till later too," Chana said.

"Chana," her mother said, sitting down at the table. "Uncle Ray may not be back for a while. He needs some time to think about things."

"Like what?" Chana asked.

"Like what he wants to do with his life," Cindi said.

"He *is* doing something with his life," Chana said. "He's painting houses and playing his drums."

"Papi wants him to have *una vida mejor*—a better life," Mrs. Millán said. "One that an education can bring. Maybe one day your uncle will have his own family, Chana. He'll need to be able to provide for them."

"But maybe he's happy here with us right now," Chana said.

"Still, an education is important. When Ray, our sisters and brothers, and I were growing up in Puerto Rico our parents—your *Abuelo* Tomás and *Abuela* Tita—barely made a living fishing. When I met your dad he encouraged me to go to college. Now I'm educated, I have a career, and I can help support my family."

"Maybe Uncle Ray doesn't like school like you did," Chana said.

Cindi stood at the counter slicing the *plátanos*. One by one, she placed them in a frying pan and Chana heard them sizzle as they hit the oil. Cindi adjusted the temperature so the pieces would brown evenly.

"As a boy in Puerto Rico, Ray loved school. But in junior high he started getting into trouble, cutting classes and playing pranks. My parents were getting on in years by then and they couldn't control him. When he was twelve they sent him to New York to live with me and your father.

"In New York, Papi and I had to be more like parents than a sister and brother-in-law to Ray. Then, when he was fourteen, you were born, Chana. He settled down and started taking school more seriously."

As Mom talked, Chana helped Cindi by salting and turning the frying *plátanos*. When they were browned on both sides, she placed them on a plate and dabbed them with a paper towel.

"When you were two, *Abuela* Tita came to help us so I could go to graduate school," Mom continued. "Uncle Ray promised *Mamá* he was going to do well. He finished high school and got accepted to college. But then *Abuela* Tita got sick and Uncle Ray took her home to Puerto Rico. She died there, when you were only four, Chana. Uncle Ray came back to New York and started working as a painter. His music helped him deal with things and he kept saying he would go back to school, but he never did. Now it's been five years and he's still searching."

"Searching for what?" Chana asked, taking the cooled slices and placing them in a *toston-era,* which was like a square, wooden, hand-held sandwich press. Chana lifted the top part, put each piece inside and pressed down with the handle, flattening it. After removing them, she gave the pieces to Cindi, who put them back in the pan to fry again.

"He's searching for what's important to him," Cindi said.

"Yes," Mom said. "And Papi pushes Ray because in college you're exposed to all kinds of careers. A degree gives you choices. We had hoped Ray would start fresh here in California. Papi is frustrated because Ray is smart. He can do anything he wants. If only he could get motivated again . . ." Mom's voice trailed off.

"Can't he do that while he's living here with us?" Chana asked. She added more salt and turned the *tostones* as they fried a second time.

"We'd like him to," Mom said. "But that's

up to Uncle Ray. He has to make some difficult decisions."

When the *tostones* were golden and crisp, Cindi removed them, patted them with paper towels, and slid them onto a clean plate. Mom took the warmed-up pizza out of the oven and the three sat down to eat.

It had been a long day. After Mrs. Millán had finished telling them Uncle Ray's story and they had eaten their dinner, Chana and Cindi went to their rooms. Chana got into bed early but promised herself she would stay awake in case she heard her uncle come in. She was still hoping he would return that night so he and Papi could resolve their difference of opinion.

Chana read until she heard her father and Clara come home and she tried to stay awake longer. She counted the glow-in-the-dark stars she and Cindi and Clara had stuck to the ceiling in her room. She tried to remember a silly *Juan Bobo* story Papi had told her once to make her laugh. She hummed her lines from a two-part song she and her uncle used to sing together, but it only made her miss him more.

Chana listened to the wind rustle the leaves on the tree outside her window and she listened for Uncle Ray's truck in the driveway. But she couldn't keep her eyes open. Finally, she snuggled deep under her blankets. She drifted off to sleep thinking about drums, and that night Chana dreamed about pennies, too.

Uncle Ray wasn't home when Chana went downstairs the next morning.

"He called and said he's staying with a friend," Papi explained to Chana and her sisters over breakfast. "He said he might be there for a while."

Chana wasn't sure who she was more angry with now, Uncle Ray or Papi. "Papi," she asked, "would you throw me out of the house if I quit school?"

"I didn't throw Ray out," Papi said, going over to Chana. He lifted her cheek in his hand and wiped away a tear with his thumb. "Your mother and I would never throw any of you out. This is your home and you're always welcome here. No matter what."

"Don't you forget that, Chana," said her mother.

Chana believed her parents, but being patient was hard. She wanted everything to be okay right now. Just then, she remembered that today was the parent-teacher conference. Chana's parents had arranged to go during their lunch breaks.

"See you at one o'clock," Mom said to Chana as she left for work. Cindi and Clara said good-bye to their mother, but they were still angry with each other and the rest of breakfast was quiet. Chana tried to make things normal again by asking Cindi and Clara, "Do you guys want an Angel Day?"

Chana and her sisters sometimes played a game Chana had made up. Chana promised not to pester them, to be an angel of a sister, for a certain amount of time. Usually, Chana could only be an angel for a day or so. On other days, Chana got Free Days from her sisters. That meant she could do anything she wanted, and her sisters couldn't tickle her or get back at her in any way for her mischief.

But this morning, Cindi and Clara only smiled at Chana and didn't say much. Papi, however, was quick to respond. "Well if they don't want one, your Mom and I will take one any day!"

"Aw, Papi!" Chana said.

Since it was parent-teacher conference day

for the fourth grade, everyone spent the morning with Mrs. Roy in the After-School Center until it was time for their turn to meet with Ms. Young. At one o'clock sharp, Mr. and Mrs. Millán arrived and they waited outside room 7 with Chana. When they went into the classroom, Mr. and Mrs. Millán shook hands with Ms. Young.

"Sanjuana is very outgoing and bright," Ms. Young said as they all sat down. "A real leader." When she asked if any of them had questions, Papi said, "Well, Chana has been a little upset about being in the lower reading group. How is she doing in reading?"

"Oh, excellent," Ms. Young assured him. "In fact, you can see on her report card here that I've given her an 'A' in reading." Ms. Young handed the report card to Papi. Then she looked at Chana and said, "You'll be moving into the Swallow group next week."

"Bravo!" Chana said.

Once they had gone over the good things they talked about where Ms. Young thought Chana could improve, which was mostly in spelling. Chana was relieved when the conference was over. Her parents thanked Ms. Young, and Chana walked outside with them.

"I never thought getting out of that reading group would be so easy," Chana said.

"Give yourself credit," her mother said. "You worked hard and showed your teacher you deserved it."

"She's not as mean as I thought she was," Chana said.

"You know, Chana," Papi said. "When you first started in Ms. Young's class, you thought she wasn't very fair. And didn't you and your friends start calling her Ms. Old?"

"Well, yeah," Chana said, feeling bad that she had made fun of her teacher.

"It's okay, *mija*," her mother said. "We're all learning how to get along here in this new town."

They had reached the car and Mom and Papi got in and said good-bye to Chana.

"Have a good afternoon at school," Papi said.

Chana was sitting at a desk reading when Mrs. Roy answered a knock at the After-School Center door. She instructed the students to continue with their activities quietly and stepped out of the room. A moment later she returned and went over to where Chana was sitting. "Chana, your uncle is here to see you," she whispered.

"Really? Can I talk to him in the hallway?" Chana asked.

"Jolly good idea," Mrs. Roy said.

Chana thanked her and went outside. "Hi! What are you doing here?" she asked anxiously.

"I came to tell you I'm sorry about yesterday. I promise I'll give you that drum lesson soon, okay?"

"You mean, you're not coming home now?" Chana asked.

"Not right now, Chana. That's another reason I came by. I know you're upset and worried. I wanted to say good-bye and tell you to remember what I told you, that we're *familia*—we'll work things out."

"When?" Chana wanted to know. "How come you're so mad at each other?"

"Oh, Chana, it's hard to explain. Your dad is trying to run my life. He wants me to go to school, and I might, but not until I'm ready."

"Mom said he just wants you to go so you can decide what to do. I mean, I always have to hear about how important school is. How come it's important for me and not for you?"

"It's important for me, too," Uncle Ray said softly.

"Mom said you already started. How come you can't just finish?" Chana asked.

"I've been meaning to. But I started school when we lived in New York. Then I had to get a job. Your dad wants me to work and go to school. It's hard."

"Well, right now you don't have to work so much. You can only paint the inside of houses in the winter, so you could go to school, too," Chana suggested.

"Yes, but I don't know what I want to study yet," Uncle Ray explained.

"Isn't that why you're supposed to go to college?" Chana asked. "To get exposed to all kinds of careers and find out? That's what Mom said."

"She's right. But we just moved and classes already started."

"But I heard Papi say they start again soon," Chana persisted.

"They do. But you have to register," Uncle Ray said.

"Can't you do that now?" Chana asked.

"Well . . ." Uncle Ray began, running out of excuses.

"Uncle Ray, don't you want to live with us

anymore?" Chana asked. She was feeling angry and sad and worried all at once, but she promised herself she wouldn't cry at school, no matter what.

"Of course I want to live with you," Chana's uncle assured her. "I just don't want your dad nagging me all the time."

"Then, if you go to school, he won't nag you," Chana reasoned.

"I will, as soon as I get around to it," Uncle Ray said, shaking his head and sighing.

"Hey, I know!" Chana said. "Let's register you now! We'll surprise Papi and tell him you're not putting it off anymore."

"I don't know, Chana," Uncle Ray protested. "Aren't you supposed to stay here at school until the regular time?"

"Yeah. But I could ask if it's okay if I go with you. If we do it today, you and Papi can make up and he won't nag you anymore," Chana said. "And I can have my drum lesson."

Uncle Ray laughed, then leaned over and mussed Chana's hair. "You're as big a nag as Hector!" He put his arm around Chana's shoulder and hugged her. "You know," he said with a smile. "I found a penny on my pillow when I went back to the house this morning to pick up some of my things. That must mean this is my lucky day."

Chana giggled, begging, "Come on, *please,* can we go now?"

Exasperated, Uncle Ray said, "*¡Ay, pestosa!* Okay, okay! I'll tell you what, kid. You stay here and I'll register for next semester at the community college."

"Right now? Promise?" Chana asked.

Uncle Ray looked at his niece then smiled and said, "Oh, okay, I promise already," and ran his finger over his chest. "Cross my heart."

He and Chana each spit a little on their index fingers, rubbed them together, shook fingertips, pulled back their hands and snapped their fingers at the same time.

"*¡Trato hecho!*" they said together. "It's a deal!"

"And tonight, Chana," Uncle Ray said before leaving. "I'll come home and talk to your dad, okay?"

"Okay!" Chana said.

Chana went back into the After-School Center room rubbing the knife in her pocket. "Pennies . ." she said to herself as she slid into her seat, "*es fuerza.*"

When the students were dismissed from the After-School Center, Chana walked to the parking lot with Stephanie, Nikki, Joy and Amanda. Stephanie's mother arrived shortly to get Stephanie. Stephanie said good-bye to her friends as she got into the car.

"*¡Viva La Squinkles!*" Stephanie yelled.

"*¡Viva La Squinkles!*" Chana and the others called back.

Joy's mother picked her up next, and then Nikki, Amanda, and Chana walked toward their houses. First they dropped off Amanda, then Chana and Nikki said good-bye in the Millán's' driveway.

Chana saw Uncle Ray's truck parked right behind her parents' car. As she walked up the front path she wasn't sure what to expect. Chana took a deep breath, climbed the porch steps, and opened the front door.

Inside, Chana could smell something delicious cooking. She headed straight for the kitchen where she could hear her mother and sisters talking and laughing. So far, so good, she thought to herself.

"Hi, sweetheart. We're having your favorite," Mrs. Millán said as Chana walked in.

"And mine, too," Uncle Ray said, coming into the kitchen behind Chana. "Pork chops with red beans and rice."

"And *tostones,*" Cindi added.

"Where's Papi?" Chana asked. "Did you make up?"

"Chana," said Uncle Ray, scooping Chana into his arms. "Your dad and I had a long talk this afternoon and we've reached a truce."

"*¡Épale!*" Chana shouted. "Right on!" She wasn't sure what a truce was, but it sounded good.

"*¡Épale!*" Papi teased her, stepping into the kitchen to join the family.

"What's a truce anyway?" Chana asked him.

"An agreement," Papi said.

"Hector," Chana's mother said to her father. "I think you and Ray should explain to the girls what happened and what you talked about."

"You're right. That's a good idea," Papi said. They sat down at the table and as they ate Papi explained.

"Your mother and I feel very strongly about school. You know, *la educación es fuerza,*" he said. Chana and her sisters rolled their eyes, but their father only smiled at them and went on. "Ray has always worked and done his share around here, and he's old enough to make his own decisions. I've been hard on him because I want him to give college some thought and not rule it out."

"School is important to me, too," Uncle Ray said to the family. "And I told Hector that I wanted to go later, when I was ready. But Chana decided I was ready now."

Everyone at the table laughed and Chana blushed.

"So we agreed that since Ray has registered and is planning to attend classes next semester, I won't be such a nag," Papi said. "Like Chana."

"Papi!" Chana said.

"It's true, you made me do it," Uncle Ray teased his niece. "I had told Hector that all his nagging was the last straw, that I was leaving for good. But thanks to you, we've talked things over."

Papi smiled and said to Chana, "That makes you the straw that broke the camel's back!"

"No," Cindi said. "She's a *straw–berry,* because she is so sweet." Cindi put a shiny penny on the table. "Chana made us think about things too," she said, pushing the penny across the table toward Chana and smiling at Clara.

"Well, what do you know?" Papi said, wrapping his big gingerbread-colored hand around Chana's. "I found one of those on my pillow last night, too."

Mom figured out what was going on and said quietly, "Our peacemaker."

"But still," Uncle Ray said. "This has been a sore spot for Hector and me for a long time. I think it would be best if we spent some time apart, so I'm going to stay with a friend for a bit. But don't worry, it's not forever."

"I think we can all live with that, don't you, Chana?" her mother asked.

"No! I don't get it," Chana said to her uncle. "I thought reaching a truce meant you were going to stay."

"We'll keep on talking and working things

out," Uncle Ray assured her. "And I owe you an apology, Chana, for not keeping my promise about giving you your drum lesson."

"It's okay," Chana said. "But I still don't understand why you can't stay."

"It's best this way, Chana," Papi said. "At least for a little while. Can you trust us on this one?"

"I guess," Chana said. She would rather Uncle Ray continued living with them, but at least he and Papi weren't fighting anymore.

"And there's more good news," Clara said.

"Yeah, Jan Jarvis is coming later on this evening to interview us—again," Cindi said, and she and Clara laughed.

Chana slipped Cindi's penny into her pocket and felt it clink against her knife. She was glad her sisters had also stopped being angry with each other.

"She said she'll be interviewing each one of us and taking photos," Mrs. Millán said.

"Maybe," Mr. Millán said, "you girls should check your rooms and make sure they look like you want them to, in case photos of you in your rooms appear in the article."

Chana and her sisters rolled their eyes again and groaned. Papi chuckled.

"Ms. Jarvis should be arriving in about an

hour," Mom said. "So we all need to start straightening up."

When Chana had finished eating, she went upstairs. As she was tidying up, her father came in.

"I thought you didn't want to clean up your room," he teased Chana.

"I don't mind. I just had to roll my eyes and groan. You know, it's a rule."

Chana's father looked puzzled and Chana said. "Papi, if I didn't do that stuff every once in a while, I'd get kicked out of the Kid Association—for sure!"

"*¡Ay, chistosa!* You're a real comic!" Papi said. He tossed his head back and gave his loud rumble-laugh that Chana loved. "And if I didn't nag every once in a while, I'd get kicked out of the Parent Association!" Papi joked back.

"Never," Chana said. "You're probably the greatest nagger in the whole United States. They must have taught you how to do that at Dad College."

"I was at the top of my class!" Papi said.

Chana giggled. Her father kissed the top of her head and said, "I'm glad you talked to your uncle, Chana. And I'm glad he talked to me. Together, we're working out our differences. I think we both needed a lesson in compromise."

Chana gave her father a big hug. When he left her room, she went back to her cleaning, in case a photo of her room appeared in the newspaper article.

"First television, and now the newspapers," Chana said to her cats. "Yes!"

When Jan Jarvis arrived at the Milláns' home, Chana greeted her at the door.

"Hi! Things are normal again," Chana said enthusiastically. "We've turned back into a warm, close-knit, Hispanic family!"

Mom's face turned as red as her hair and Papi cleared his throat several times, sounding as if something were caught there. "Ms. Jarvis!" he said loudly. "It's so nice to see you. Please come in."

As Mom led Jan Jarvis into the living room, Papi pulled Chana aside. "I want an Angel Day starting right this second!" he said with a laugh.

Cindi and Uncle Ray were already seated in the living room. Clara came in and served juice and the pastries Chana and Mrs. Millán had bought the day before.

To Chana, it seemed like they talked about boring, grown-up things for a long time. "Yes," Mrs. Millán was saying, "the commute to work is certainly nicer than in the city."

"Of course, we're very happy with the public schools our daughters are in," Papi said.

"Kids here drive their own cars to school," Clara mentioned. "In New York, we just took the subway."

"I really like living around so many trees and parks. And baseball fields that are grass instead of cement," Cindi said.

"I'm excited about all the popular clubs in the area. Especially the ones around the college campus," Uncle Ray said. "I'm planning to put a band together, Ms. Jarvis."

"Oh, you can call me J.J.," Jan Jarvis said, blushing.

Uncle Ray and Jan Jarvis grinned at each other and Chana wondered if her uncle was going to ask "J.J." out on a date.

"My uncle is a great drummer," Chana told her, smiling at Uncle Ray. "He has a kit and everything and he's teaching me," she said. "Want us to play for you?"

"Definitely!" Jan Jarvis said. "I love good salsa."

In the garage, Chana and Uncle Ray each played the drums for their guest. Jan Jarvis took several pictures of them and even tried playing a bit herself.

"Jammin' J.J.!" Uncle Ray said as she banged and crashed away.

Afterward, the twins gave her a tour of the rest of the house and then Chana invited her into her room. She showed her all her dollmaking things, including the thread she used and the buttons and trinkets she collected for their outfits. Chana showed her the Squinkles T-shirt she had made, and showed off her books and her cats and the tall tree outside her window.

Jan Jarvis took pictures of each of the girls in her room. Back downstairs, the adults began talking again.

"Do you have more family in California?" Jan Jarvis asked Papi. "Other than your brother in San Diego."

"Not yet," answered Papi.

"But we're going to have a whole house full of relatives here at the end of the month for the holidays," Mrs. Millán said.

"That sounds like fun," Jan Jarvis said.

"Yes, we're hoping more of the family will move out here. We like it very much," Papi said.

"It's our Aunt Media who's coming," Clara said. "And our cousins."

"Her real name is Una," Mom said with a chuckle.

"But she's so skinny we started calling her Media instead of Una when we were kids," Uncle Ray told Jan Jarvis.

Everyone burst into laughter because in Spanish, *una* meant one, and *media* meant half. When Cindi explained this to Jan Jarvis, she started laughing, too.

Before leaving, Jan Jarvis took a picture of the whole family, including Flaca and Sparky, on the living room sofa. Then she put her notebook and camera in her bag and stood up to shake hands with everyone.

"Let me get your coat," Uncle Ray said.

"Thank you, Ray," Jan Jarvis said. At the door she added, "It was great meeting all of you. I think this edition of New Faces is going to be my best one yet."

Mrs. Millán thanked her for coming and Jan Jarvis said, "My pleasure. And if I meet

my deadline, you can find this article in Sunday's paper."

Everyone shouted their good-byes from the porch.

Back inside, Chana and her sisters started teasing their uncle.

"She was *really* nice, wasn't she, Uncle Ray?" Cindi said.

"I didn't see a wedding band on her finger," Clara commented.

Ray only smiled until Chana said, "J.J., let me get your coat for you," and made loud kissing noises. Ray started to chase the girls but they each ran in a different direction, laughing and screaming. Chana darted upstairs before he could catch her.

"Good night!" she called when she had reached the safety of her room.

Chana put on her pajamas and got into bed with a book she had selected from her bookshelf. She arranged herself so she could read comfortably, and as she did she found a small piece of paper under one of her pillows.

In neat handwriting, with a perfect drawing of a sparkling red drum set in the corner, Chana read: Good for drum lessons. Offer valid forever.

Chana smiled. *"La familia . . . es fuerza,"* she said to Flaca. She put the coupon on her nightstand beside the penny and her knife. Then Chana opened her book and began reading one of her favorite stories.

Abuela/Abuelo: Grandmother, grandfather
Adiós: Good-bye
Apodo: Nickname
¡Ay!: Oh!
¡Ay, chistosa!: You're a real comic (female)
Barrio: Neighborhood
¡Bravo!: Hooray!
Bon appétit: Enjoy the meal (French)
Buen provecho: Enjoy the meal (Spanish)
Buon appetito: Enjoy the meal (Italian)
Bueno: Good
¡Cállate!: Quiet!
Cálmate: Calm down
¡Caramba!: Oh, darn! Oh, man!
¡Dios mío!: My goodness!
El Gigante: the Giant

¡El último que llegue es un huevo podrido!: Last one there is a rotten egg
¡Épale!: Right on!
Escuincle/escuincles: Little kid(s)
Estoy preocupada: I'm worried
Familia: Family
Flaca: Skinny (female)
Gracias, Tío: Thank you, Uncle
Hija: Daughter
¡Híjole!: Oh, my gosh! Wow!
Juan Bobo: A fictional "noodlehead" character popular in Puerto Rican folktales
La educación es fuerza: Education is strength
Loca: Crazy (female)
Los Gigantes: the Giants
Media: Half (female)
Mija: My daughter (mi hija), little one
¡Nos vemos, cocodrilo!: See ya later, alligator! (cocodrilo means crocodile but the expression is used in the same way)
¡Órale!: Right on!
Paella: A fish, chicken and rice casserole dish that originated in Spain
Pestosa: Pest (female)
Pasale: Come in
Plátanos: Raw, fat, green type of bananas (used in soups, desserts, fried, and baked)
Por nada: You're welcome

Pronto: Pretty soon
¡Qué nice!: How nice!
¿Qué pasa?: What's up? What's the matter?
¡Qué rico!: How delicious!
Seguro que sí: Definitely
Sí ¡Y orgullosa!: Yes. And proud!
¡Trato hecho!: It's a deal!
Tostones: Twice-fried green bananas (when raw they are called *plátanos*)
Una: One (female)
Una vida mejor: A better life
Vámonos: Let's go!
¡Viva La Squinkles!: Long Live the Squinkles

LEE COUNTY LIBRARY SYSTEM
3 3262 00178 3551